PUFFIN BOOKS

THE STRAWBERRY-JAM PONY

Tommy can't believe it when his big brother Norman asks for his help with the pit ponies. Norman is old enough to work down the mine driving the ponies, but Tommy must wait another *five* years! Then the miners come out on strike and the ponies have to be brought up to the surface. They need all the riders they can get, so Tommy willingly helps out. His favourite pony is Gleam, who loves strawberry-jam sandwiches.

The ponies are delighted at being out in the fresh air and daylight, but their existence is suddenly put under threat ... and only Tommy's plan has a chance of saving them!

This is an exciting and evocative story.

Sheila Lavelle was born in Gateshead, County Durham, and has been writing since she was at school. She now lives in a cottage near the sea in Galloway, Scotland, with her husband and two border collies. Sheila's mornings are spent writing, and then in the afternoons she walks the dogs. Her many interests include reading, bird-watching, spinning and weaving, and classical music (especially Italian opera).

THE STRAWBERRY-JAM PONY

by
SHEILA LAVELLE

Illustrated by Valerie Littlewood

PUFFIN BOOKS

To my dear uncle,
the real Norman Wilson

PUFFIN BOOKS

Published by the Penguin Group
Penguin Books Ltd, 27 Wrights Lane, London W8 5TZ, England
Penguin Books USA Inc., 375 Hudson Street, New York, New York 10014, USA
Penguin Books Australia Ltd, Ringwood, Victoria, Australia
Penguin Books Canada Ltd, 10 Alcorn Avenue, Toronto, Ontario, Canada M4V 3B2
Penguin Books (NZ) Ltd, 182–190 Wairau Road, Auckland 10, New Zealand

Penguin Books Ltd, Registered Offices: Harmondsworth, Middlesex, England

First published by Hamish Hamilton 1987
Published in Puffin Books 1989
5 7 9 10 8 6 4

Text copyright © Sheila Lavelle, 1987
Illustrations copyright © Valerie Littlewood, 1987
All rights reserved

Printed in England by Clays Ltd, St Ives plc
Filmset in Baskerville

Chapter 1

THE BEST DAY of Tommy Wilson's life was the day he saw the strawberry-jam pony for the very first time. He didn't know when he woke up in the morning that anything special was going to happen. In fact, he didn't want to wake up at all.

It was his brother Norman's candle shining into his eyes that disturbed him, and he groaned and buried his head under the blankets.

"Sorry, Tommy," whispered Norman. Tommy felt the springs creak as his brother climbed out of the folding bed which they shared in the kitchen of the cottage.

"What's up, Norm?" yawned Tommy, pulling the covers off his head and rubbing his eyes. "It's the middle of the bloomin' night."

Norman lit the gas lamp over the fireplace and blew out the candle.

"It's five o'clock, stupid," he said. "I've got to be at work by half-past, to feed the ponies before they start their shift." He washed himself briefly at the tap in the scullery and then began to pull on his clothes.

Sitting up in bed, Tommy watched enviously as his brother laced up his boots and settled his cap at a jaunty angle on his head. The year was 1926 and Norman was fourteen, old enough to work in the coal-mine, driving the ponies that pulled the tubs of coal. It

didn't seem fair to Tommy that he was only nine, and had five more years to wait.

Tommy groaned at the thought. Five more years of that rotten school, where they rapped your knuckles with a ruler if you forgot your nine-times table, while your brother rode ponies all day and earned eight shillings a week. It wasn't fair at all.

Norman packed his dinner-bag with the bread and cheese and the bottle of cold tea which their mother had left out for him the night before. Then he stood at the table and cut four more slices from the loaf. Two of these he spread with margarine and ate for his breakfast, and the other two he sandwiched together with strawberry jam from a jar at the back of the pantry. Tommy whistled and his eyes grew round.

"Norman!" he said. "That jam's for Dad's tea. I'll tell Mam."

Norman wrapped the sandwich in a bit of newspaper and shoved it into his bag.

"Oh, Tommy, don't tell," he said. "It's for Gleam, the new pony. He'll do anything for a bit of strawberry jam."

Both lads looked up towards the ceiling at a sound from the bedroom upstairs, where their mother slept with their three-year-old sister Maggie, and where their father would sleep when he came home from night-shift at the pit.

"I won't tell, if you give me a penny for a comic," said Tommy with a crafty grin, and his brother scowled at him as they heard their mother coming down the stairs.

"You little stinker!" he said. "I only get sixpence a week pocket-money."

"Mam!" called Tommy. "Our Norm's been . . . *oof*!" His voice was suddenly cut off as Norman clamped his hand over his mouth.

"Twerp!" said Norman, flinging a coin at Tommy's head. He slung his bag over his shoulder, grabbed his driver's whip from behind the dresser, and ran for the door, just as their mother came into the kitchen in her

dressing-gown, her hair in a long plait down her back.

"Tarra, Mam. See you later," shouted Norman. Then the door banged and he was gone.

"Norman's a good lad," said Tommy's mother, filling the kettle and lighting the gas under it. "His wages come in real handy. I hope you'll work as hard when you're fourteen, Tommy."

Tommy bounced gleefully about on the bed, his penny clutched in his hand.

"I will, Mam," he promised. "I can hardly wait to get a pony of me own to look after."

Tommy's wish was to come true sooner than he expected. An hour later, when the bed had been folded away and a coal fire was burning in the grate,

Tommy sat at the kitchen table in his nightshirt, eating porridge with Maggie. His mother, frying a bit of bacon for their father's breakfast, kept looking at the clock with a worried frown on her face.

"It's not like your Dad to be this late," she said. Then she dropped the spoon and put her hands over her ears as a horrible wailing noise suddenly filled the room.

Maggie spilt her porridge and started to cry. Tommy's mother moved towards the door, her face turning pale.

"It's the pit siren," she said. "It means there's been an accident. What if your dad . . . ?"

The door suddenly opened and Tommy's father strode in, his face grim under its covering of coal-dust. He took

9

his trembling wife in his arms and patted her shoulder awkwardly while she sobbed against his chest.

"There, there, bonny lass. It's all right," he said. "The siren's not announcing a disaster. This time it's announcing a triumph."

Tommy's mother wiped her eyes on her apron. "What do you mean, Joe?" she said. "Are the bosses giving you more money at last?"

Her husband sat down at the fire and began to pull off his boots. "Nay, lass," he said. "They're much too greedy for that. They've turned us down, yet again."

He peeled off his damp socks and draped them over the fender to dry. "Well, they've had it their own way long enough," he said. "There's been a meeting this morning, and the lads

have agreed to go on strike. There'll not be one shovel of coal dug out of that mine until we get more pay. The pit's closed, and lord knows when it'll be open again." And he folded his arms and stared moodily into the flames.

Maggie slipped down from her chair and ran to climb into her father's lap. Tommy's mother began to pour out the tea.

"The ponies, Dad!" burst out Tommy, standing by the door with his mouth open. "What will happen to the ponies?"

Just then Norman rushed in, his cap crooked and his hair sticking out round his head.

"Hey, Tommy!" he shouted, grinning all over his face. "Get your clothes on, man. The ponies are coming up out of the pit, and we need all the riders we

12

can get." Then he turned and dashed
out again.

Tommy didn't need telling twice.
Not bothering to wash, he scrambled
into his clothes, flung on his cap and
made for the door.

"Wait a minute, Tommy," called his mother. "What about school?"

But Tommy didn't stop. "Hang school!" he muttered under his breath. "I've got better things to do." And he raced off down the street after his brother.

Chapter 2

TOMMY HURRIED THROUGH the village towards the coal-mine near the sea. Then he suddenly stopped dead as he turned the last corner and the pit-head came into view. His eyes widened and an enormous grin spread over his face at the marvellous sight before his eyes.

Between twenty and thirty ponies were trotting towards him along the cobbled road. Black ponies, grey ponies, chestnut ponies, ponies dappled white and brown, they all had the docked tails and close-shaven coats and leather head-gear of the working pit-pony. Excited by the daylight and the

fresh air, they tossed their heads and twitched their ears at the people who came out to watch them go by.

In front, riding bareback on a strong black mare and leading another by the bridle, was a thin-faced man with a

moustache. It was Norman's boss, Mr
Gibson, the stable-keeper at the mine.
He was a friend of Tommy's father, and
Tommy knew him well.

"Now then," shouted Mr Gibson.
"Come to give us a hand, have you?"

He chuckled at Tommy's beaming face. "Tell Norman to let you have Gleam," he said. "He's a grand pony, that. Won't give you no bother."

Tommy watched the ponies and their riders clatter by until he caught sight of his brother riding along next to Albert, his skinny, ginger-haired friend. Norman's pony was a frisky grey, which needed all his strength to control, making it difficult for him to hold on to the reins of the brown pony that trotted alongside.

"Tommy!" called Norman. "Look after Gleam, will you? I can't manage him as well as this awkward beggar."

He threw the brown pony's reins into Tommy's hands. "Ride 'im, Tommy," he grinned. "Or you can just lead him if you like. And here, carry this dinner-bag for me as well."

He pulled the bag from his shoulder and flung it down, then dug in his heels and cantered briskly away.

Tommy picked up the bag and put his arm through the strap. He held the pony's bridle and stared after his brother. All he knew about riding horses was from watching Tom Mix in

cowboy films at the Empire Picture House on Saturdays. He'd never ridden a real horse in his life before, although he had dreamed about it often enough. And here was that daft Norman telling him to ride, as if it was the easiest thing in the world. The bloomin' thing didn't even have a saddle.

The pony stood patiently in the road while Tommy let the others go past. The people went back into their houses, the siren stopped wailing, and the street became suddenly quiet. Tommy gazed at the pony, admiring its glossy coat, the white blaze on its face, and the intelligent look in its eyes.

"Now then, Gleam," he murmured softly.

The pony stared into Tommy's face for a moment. Then something happened that made Tommy almost burst

with happiness. With a whinny of pleasure, the pony stepped forward, placed
its chin on Tommy's shoulder and
gently nuzzled his ear.

Tommy glowed all over as if he'd just
eaten a bowl of his granny's best beef
stew with dumplings. It was better than
the time he got a second-hand bicycle
from his father for Christmas, and
even better than scoring that amazing

final goal which had once won the football cup for his school team.

He put his arms around the pony's neck and gave him a hug. Then, grabbing a handful of mane in one hand, and clutching the reins in the other, he managed to scramble awkwardly onto his back.

Tommy nudged Gleam's sides with his heels and clicked his tongue.

"Trot on, Gleam," he said. And, to his delight and amazement, the pony trotted forward over the cobbles, following the route the others had taken.

Tommy was bounced about so much that his teeth rattled in his head as the pony, anxious to catch up with his comrades, cantered through the village. Several times he almost tumbled off, and once he bashed his head on a tree, which made him say a very bad word.

But by clinging tightly to the mane with both hands, he somehow managed to stay on until the other ponies came in sight.

The rest of the group was only a short way ahead when a stone, flung by someone standing on the pavement, suddenly knocked Tommy's cap flying into the road. Other stones followed, stinging his legs and body and striking the terrified pony, who shied sideways and snorted down his nostrils in fright.

"What an old nag!" shouted a jeering voice, and Tommy's heart sank into his boots when he saw that it was Danny Bates, leader of the worst bunch of bullies you could meet.

Danny and his gang were thirteen years old and the terror of the school playground. Their hideout was in a spooky old house called Askew Hall on the cliffs near the sea. Nobody else dared go there, for the Hall was supposed to be haunted by the ghosts of the Three Sisters. People said that three young nuns had been chained up and left there to die many years before. But others said that it was all rubbish, and that the house had once been used by smugglers, who had started the rumours to frighten everybody away.

Many scary tales were told of secret passages, skeletons in the cellars, and strange noises at night. But Danny and his gang only laughed at such stories. They camped out at the Hall during summer weekends, and had wild parties there, safe from prying eyes.

Danny's idea of having fun was to torment anyone smaller than himself, and it was just Tommy's bad luck that he should bump into him now.

With a red face and sweating hands Tommy struggled to control his pony, and he almost sobbed with relief when he heard hoofbeats on the cobbles and

saw his brother galloping back to look
for him. After taking one look at Norman's snorting pony charging fiercely
towards him, Danny Bates disappeared
rapidly round the corner.

Norman reined in the grey pony and
spoke quietly to Gleam until he calmed
down. Then he slid to the ground and
picked up Tommy's cap from the road.

"What's been going on?" he said. "Giving you some bother was he, that Danny Bates?"

Tommy managed a grin.

"I'm all right," he said. "It was Gleam I was worried about."

Norman gazed at him proudly.

"You're a brave lad," he said, and Tommy felt ten feet tall. "I knew you'd manage, if I let you get on with it by yourself. What do you think of Gleam, then?"

"He's grand!" Tommy burst out. "But I haven't half got a sore bum!"

Norman laughed. "Try gripping with your knees," he advised. "Then you won't bounce so much. We're taking them to the Banky Field. It's not far now."

The two brothers trotted their ponies side by side along the lane out of the village and up the hillside. The sun was stronger now, the air felt warm, and the ponies began to quicken their pace at the sight of green fields ahead.

Chapter 3

THE BANKY FIELD was a patch of grassy land about half a mile from the village. Tommy often went there for picnics, or to fly his kite on windy afternoons with his friend Billy Snaith. The air always seemed cool and clean on the hill above the sea, and there was plenty of fresh grass. Tommy knew that a better place for the ponies would be hard to find.

The ponies jogged on until they reached a wooden gate in the hedge. Mr Gibson untied the bit of rope which fastened the gate, and stood back to let everybody through.

29

"Here we are, lads," he said, smiling. "Take the ponies' bridles off and chuck all the gear into that old barn. Then let the blighters go."

Tommy slid stiffly from his pony's back, staggering when his feet hit the ground.

"Ow!" he groaned, clutching his behind. "I won't be able to sit down for a week."

"Watch where you're putting your feet," laughed the stable-keeper, and Tommy groaned again when he saw what he had landed in.

"Never mind," grinned Norman. "Horse-muck makes grand manure. Maybe it'll make you grow, like Grandad's rhubarb."

Tommy scowled and stuck his tongue out, which made Norman laugh even more.

"Listen, lads," said Mr Gibson. "I've got to go to London for a few days to a union meeting, and I want somebody sensible to keep an eye on the ponies while I'm gone. Feed and groom them every day, and stop them running too wild, like. You'll be in charge, Norman, with your mate Albert, and I'll pick half a dozen others as well." He looked at Tommy thoughtfully. "What about you, Tom? Do you want to help?"

Tommy felt so pleased he could hardly speak. "I . . . er . . . yes, please, Mr Gibson!" he blurted out. But Norman shook his head.

"Tommy has to go to school, Mr Gibson," he said. "Mam will never let him miss his lessons." Tommy glared at his brother and aimed a kick at his shin.

The stable-keeper chuckled. "That's all right, Tom," he said. "You can come every morning before school, and then again in the afternoons. Look after Gleam, as he seems to have taken a fancy to you. Norman will show you how to do things right." He turned and led his own pony away into the field.

Norman showed Tommy how to unbuckle Gleam's bridle and take the bit out of his mouth. All around them other men and boys were doing the same thing, slapping the ponies' backs and sending them off into the meadow to graze.

Tommy watched them, his eyes shining. In their first few moments of freedom after months of working underground, the ponies went wild with delight. They bucked and pranced and tossed their heads, they rolled on their backs and kicked their legs in the air, and they galloped madly backwards

and forwards over the grass, whinnying for joy.

"Off you go, Gleam," said Tommy, patting his pony's neck.

But the pony didn't seem keen to join the others. He kept pressing as close as possible to Tommy's side, snuffling at the dinner-bag which he still wore over his shoulder.

Norman grinned. "The crafty beggar!" he exclaimed. "He can smell the jam. He wants his sandwich. Don't you, Gleam, me bonny lad?"

Tommy opened the bag and took out the parcel. But before he could even begin to unwrap it, Gleam had pushed his nose into the paper, bumping Tommy backwards with his head, and whinnying eagerly at the scent of his favourite food.

Tommy got the wrapping off at last, and held the bread and jam out towards the pony. Gleam's ears twitched and his eyes rolled as he took it into his mouth and began to chew. Tommy and Norman looked at one another and smiled.

The sandwich finished, Gleam turned and cantered away over the field. Tommy stuffed his hands into his pockets and felt suddenly miserable.

Norman gave him a shove. "Hey, cheer up," he said. "You can come up for half an hour at dinner-time. But you'd better get off to school now. It must be well after nine o'clock."

There was nothing Tommy could do but obey, so with a last look at the ponies, he trudged off down the hill towards the village.

Miss Potts was Tommy's teacher. She was short and dark with fat legs

and a bad temper, and she didn't seem to like children at all. She certainly didn't like dirty children who came into school late with horse-muck on their boots, and she made Tommy take them off and leave them outside the door.

Tommy didn't care. All he could think about was his pony, waiting for

him at the Banky Field, and he counted the minutes until twelve o'clock.

The bell rang at last. Tommy pulled on his boots and raced down the corridor to the boys' cloakroom to get his coat.

"Coming down the beach after dinner, Tommy?" asked Billy Snaith, taking his cap from the peg next to Tommy's. "We could take a candle this time, and have a proper look at that secret tunnel."

They had found the tunnel the day before, while playing hide and seek in the caves along the beach. Looking for a good hiding-place, Tommy had heaved away a big rock from the back of a cave. And there it was, a dark, narrow passage, leading deep into the cliff, and just begging to be explored.

Tommy had been waiting for a

chance to go back there with a light, to find out where the secret passage led. But today he had more important things to do.

"Sorry, Billy," he said, swaggering towards the door. "I've got to go and ride my horse." And he ran gleefully out into the yard, giggling at Billy's astonished face.

Tommy's mother tutted in annoyance when Tommy burst into the house and begged for strawberry-jam sandwiches for his dinner.

"What about this lovely mince and dumplings?" she said crossly, stirring a pot on the stove. "It's your favourite. I made it specially." But Tommy pleaded so hard that at last she gave in, on condition that he washed his face and cleaned his smelly boots before going out again.

Tommy got away as soon as he could. He ran all the way up the hill to the Banky Field, clutching the sandwiches in his hand. He reached the gate at last, and scrambled over it to save time.

The ponies were frisking about in a corner of the field. Tommy was about to shout Gleam's name when he saw a brown pony leave the others and start galloping towards him across the grass. He laughed out loud as he realised it was Gleam.

"Good lad!" he said, when Gleam skidded to a halt in front of him, snorting and pawing the ground. "Look what I've brought for our dinner."

Soon he and his pony were happily munching their sandwiches together. Tommy thought that strawberry jam had never tasted so good.

Chapter 4

EVERY MORNING for the next few days, Tommy got up at dawn and ran off to the Banky Field to spend as much time as possible with Gleam before school. And as soon as school was over at twelve o'clock he would race home, grab his sandwiches, and rush away up the hill.

"That bairn's bewitched," complained Tommy's dad, staring sourly into the fire with nothing to do. "It'll break his heart when the strike's over, and that pony has to go back down the pit."

"Oh, leave him be," said Tommy's
mother. "It could be another six
months yet. Let him enjoy it while he
can."

Most of all Tommy loved the long
summer evenings. He had from four
o'clock until bedtime to spend as he

pleased, and there was always plenty to do. The ponies had to be fed and groomed and exercised, and the best way to exercise them was to ride them.

Every evening after tea, Tommy and Norman and a few of Norman's friends would mount the ponies and gallop bareback around the fields until dark. Whooping and yelling and shouting with excitement, they would chase each other over the grass, playing bandits, or highwaymen, or cowboys, their favourite game of all. The ponies enjoyed all the fun , and soon the fresh air, exercise and daily grooming made their coats shine with health and fitness.

Gleam didn't like anyone to ride him but Tommy. He would wait by the gate snorting impatiently until Tommy arrived, and would whinny with joy when he saw him running up the hill.

The only thing that spoilt it all was Danny Bates's gang. Several times they turned up to sneer and throw stones, and once they even let all the ponies out to roam the village and trample in people's gardens, which got Norman and his friends into a lot of trouble.

"That's it," said Norman grimly, after wasting almost the whole evening rounding the ponies up again. "We'd better not leave them on their own any more." From then on he and Albert took blankets and a stove and camped out in the barn.

Saturday came at last and there was no school. Tommy threw on his clothes, swallowed his breakfast, then hunted about under the sink until he found an old tin pail.

"Going up that Banky Field again, are you?" grumbled Tommy's dad. "You'll fall off that pony one of these days and break your blinkin' neck."

"I'm going down the beach first," said Tommy. "To get some winkles." His sister Maggie screwed up her face and began to wail.

"Take her with you, Tommy," said

his mother, and Tommy scowled. Tommy hated taking Maggie out with him. She always had a snotty nose and she never stopped whining.

"Aw, Mam," he groaned. "Do I have to? She wet her knickers the last time."

Tommy's father stood up and took one step towards him.

"All right, I'll take her," said Tommy hastily. "Come on, Maggie. Get your bonnet on."

Tommy's mother slipped something into his pocket as they were leaving. It was a small packet of sandwiches, and Tommy knew that in them was the last of the strawberry jam. With his dad on strike, there would be no money for any more, and that was why he had thought up the winkle plan.

Maggie insisted on bringing her own small bucket and spade, and Tommy

held her hand as they trudged down
to the beach. He had timed it just
right. The tide was out and the
best winkles could be found in the
pools among the rocks. In the end
he was glad he had brought Maggie
with him, for she soon grew tired
of digging in the sand, and came

to help. She was good at finding the winkles among the seaweed, and in no time at all they had filled Tommy's pail to the brim, and Maggie's little bucket as well.

"What we gonna do?" said Maggie, as Tommy lugged the heavy pail over the rocks. "We gonna cook them and eat them up?"

"Not likely," said Tommy. "We're going to sell them."

Maggie stamped her foot and howled. "Me wanna eat them with a pin!" she yelled in fury.

Tommy didn't bother to argue with her. He set off up the beach, carrying the pail of winkles towards Appleby's shop. Maggie trailed along behind, still howling.

Appleby's was the sort of shop that sold everything — gobstoppers and shoelaces, candles and tummy-pills, stotty cakes and baked beans. Mrs Appleby, a fat woman with a red face and a cough, was weighing biscuits on a pair of brass scales. She leaned over the counter when she saw Maggie, and put half a broken biscuit into her hand. Maggie stopped yelling at once.

"Poor bairn's hungry," wheezed Mrs Appleby, coughing with the effort of standing up. "Hello, Tommy. What can I get you today?"

Tommy held up his pail. "Do you want to buy some fresh winkles, Missus?" he said. "You could boil them and sell them in the shop. I bet you could make a nice profit, an' all."

Mrs Appleby peered down at the winkles. "Well, I suppose I could," she said. "But that would depend on what you're asking for them, wouldn't it?"

"Not much," said Tommy, grinning his cheeky grin that his mam said could charm sparrows out of trees. "I only want a jar of strawberry jam."

Mrs Appleby had such a fit of coughing that she almost choked.

"Good lad," she wheezed, dabbing her eyes. "Helping the family while your dad's on strike, are you? Earning jam for your little sister's bread?"

Maggie sniffed and wiped her nose on her sleeve. "It's not for me," she said. "It's for that daft horsie . . . Ow!" She hopped up and down as Tommy trod hard on her foot.

"Shurrup, stupid!" he hissed in her ear, and luckily Mrs Appleby didn't seem to have heard. To Tommy's relief she reached up and took a jar of strawberry jam from the shelf. Still wheezing and muttering, she wrapped it up in a

53

small piece of newspaper and handed it over the counter.

"Thanks, Missus," grinned Tommy, shoving it into the deep pocket of his jacket. Then he grabbed Maggie's hand and pulled her out of the shop. He almost dragged her up the lane towards home, and bundled her and her bucket through the door without listening to her yells.

"Me wanna sell *my* winkles too," bawled Maggie, kicking at his ankles in the kitchen. "Me gonna tell Mam!"

Luckily Tommy's mother was upstairs, and there was no sign of his dad. Pausing only long enough to stuff his spare pocket with a few slices of bread, Tommy ran out again. He was so pleased with the success of his winkle plan that he almost flew up the hill to the Banky Field. Now he had a whole jarful of strawberry jam for Gleam, not just one measly sandwich.

Tommy jumped up and down as he ran alongside the hedge, hoping for a glimpse of the pony. But for once Gleam was not in his usual place by the gate.

Surprised to see only a few ponies in the field, Tommy climbed the gate and looked anxiously around.

"He must be behind the barn, or something," Tommy told himself, with a strange cold feeling in his chest.

Gleam was not behind the barn. He was nowhere in the field at all, and Tommy's heart beat fast as he stared helplessly about.

A shout from the barn doorway made him look round. He hardly knew the two battered figures that limped slowly towards him. Their faces scratched and bloody, their clothes filthy and torn they looked as if they'd had a fight with a tiger and lost.

"Norman!" cried Tommy, his voice coming out in a squeak. "And Albert! What happened? Where's the rest of the ponies? And where's Gleam?"

Norman held a hanky to his bloody

nose and peered at Tommy out of puffed-up eyes.

"It was that stinkin' Danny Bates and his lot," he muttered thickly. "The lousy rotters beat us up. They took ten of our best ponies and went off with them."

"We couldn't do nowt to stop them," Albert put in, his knobbly knees sticking out through rips in his trousers. "They came in the night. There was ten of them and only two of us."

Tommy stared at his brother. "What do they want them for?" he demanded. "Are they going to ride them?"

"I suppose so," sighed Norman, kicking moodily at a clump of grass with his boot. "They're calling themselves 'The Masked Riders'. They'll be galloping around the village like hooligans, I expect."

Tommy went cold all over when he thought of those great bullies riding Gleam.

"Not if I can help it, they won't!" he shouted fiercely. And he raced off along the cliff-path towards Danny's hideout.

Chapter 5

TOMMY STOOD OUTSIDE the padlocked
iron gates of Askew Hall, gasping for
breath after running all the way. He
peered through the rusty metalwork at
the overgrown drive and the ivy-
covered stone building beyond. There
was no sign of any ponies, but faint
neighing sounds reached his ears from
somewhere inside.

There came a sudden shout from
behind the gate, and a bit of sharp rock
struck Tommy in the chest. Two of
Danny's gang were standing in the
drive, armed with catapults and hand-
fuls of stones.

59

"Clear off, Tommy Wilson!" one of them called. "Them ponies are where you or nobody else can't get at them."

"Danny's locked them in the cellar," yelled the other, grinning spitefully and hurling another stone. "The butcher's coming tomorrow, to turn them all into horse-meat. And we've got the whole place guarded, so you might as well get lost, you stinkin' little twerp."

Tommy's face went white. "I'll kick your teeth in if you hurt my pony," he shouted back, rattling the gates furiously with both hands. He would have tried to climb over if Norman and Albert, who had followed him along the cliff-top, hadn't suddenly appeared and dragged him away.

"Calm down, Tommy," panted Norman. "Screeching like an old witch won't get you nowhere." He pulled Tommy behind the high stone wall which surrounded the house, and all three flung themselves on the ground to get their breath back.

"They're having you on," said Norman grimly, when Tommy had gasped out what he'd heard. "Danny wouldn't dare. He'd be in trouble with the mine owners, and even the cops, if he sold the ponies for horse-meat."

Tommy wasn't so sure. That Danny Bates was horrible enough for anything. They had to get the ponies back, and it had to be soon.

"We've got to do something, Norm," he urged. "Fetch the rest of the lads. Get stones . . . and sticks and things. Knock the door down and kick that stupid Danny right up the backside."

"It would take an army," said Albert, looking at the solid wall and the heavy gates. "That place is built like a fort. And we don't want a bloody battle with that lot. Some of the ponies might get hurt. We'll have to think of something a bit cleverer than that."

Tommy rolled over and pressed his face into the grass. His throat went dry as he thought of Gleam being taken away and turned into horse-meat.

"Why don't we get our Dad," he choked out angrily, after a moment. "I bet he wouldn't half sort them out."

Norman shook his head. "He'd only tell us to fight our own battles and not be such sissies," he replied, and Tommy knew he was right.

Albert sighed miserably. "We'll have to wait for Mr Gibson to get back," he said. "But I don't know what he's gonna say. He trusted us to look after them ponies."

Tommy jumped to his feet.

"We can't sit here all day and do nowt," he shouted. "Climb the wall . . . or dig a tunnel . . . or something."

Albert suddenly sat up with a strange look on his freckled face.

"A tunnel . . . " he said slowly. "Wait

a minute . . . Crikey! There is a tunnel. Them smugglers are supposed to have made it, ages ago. It goes from a secret opening in the cellars of the house, down through the cliff to the sea. Mr Gibson's grandad told him about it, when he was a kid."

Norman grabbed his friend's arm. "Why, man, the entrance must be down there somewhere on the beach," he said excitedly. "In one of them caves. Did Mr Gibson say where it was?"

Albert shook his head gloomily. "The tunnel's been lost for a hundred years," he said. "Nobody even knows which cave it's in."

Tommy had been standing there all this time with his mouth open like a penguin who'd dropped its fish. He gulped hard and his voice wobbled when he spoke.

"I do," he told them, and they both stared at him, astonished. "I know which cave it's in." And he turned and dashed off down the cliff-path towards the beach, with Norman and Albert not far behind.

They scrambled down the steep rocky slope and were soon running along the beach to the group of caves at the far end.

"It's in this one," said Tommy, hopping from one foot to the other with excitement. "The one with the pile of pebbles at the entrance. I put them there so I wouldn't forget."

At the back of the cave, Norman helped Tommy to roll away the rock which hid the opening to the tunnel. There was just enough light in the cave for them to see that a passage did indeed go deep into the side of the cliff, and that it sloped upwards after the first few yards.

"Wow, Tommy!" breathed Norman. "I reckon this is it, all right. Look, it goes straight up towards the Hall."

"And if Mr Gibson's grandad was

right," Albert put in, his eyes gleaming in the gloom, "it'll bring us out right inside the cellars, where them blighters are keeping our ponies."

Tommy was all for rushing into the tunnel straight away, but Norman held him back.

"Don't be daft," he said sensibly.

"We need some sort of light, for a start. And don't forget they may be guarding the cellars." He pulled Tommy back out into the sunshine.

"Listen," he said. "We'll wait until tonight, when they're asleep. They won't be expecting an attack then, and we'll take them by surprise."

"Great!" said Tommy, jigging up and down with glee. But Norman's next words wiped the grin from his face at once.

"You needn't think you're coming," he said. "You're far too little for this kind of trouble. I'll get some of me biggest mates to help. You can stay at home in bed." And no matter how hard Tommy begged and pleaded, Norman refused to listen.

Albert's face had gone pale, and he looked far from happy at the idea.

"Hey, Norm," he muttered, shuffling his feet on the pebbles. "I don't fancy that place in the middle of the night. It's supposed to be haunted. What about them ghosts, man? What if we bump into them Three Sisters?"

Norman laughed out loud at Albert's horrified face. But it was the mention of the word ghosts that gave Tommy an idea.

Chapter 6

TOMMY FELT SOMEONE shaking his shoulder, and woke up with a start.

"Ssh!" hissed Norman, a hand over Tommy's mouth. "It's twelve o'clock. Get your clothes on, kid. And for Pete's sake don't wake Mam and Dad."

Tommy was wide awake in an instant, his heart thumping with excitement. The moon shone through the window, giving him just enough light to find his clothes. He pulled on his shirt and trousers, and then his jacket, patting the pocket to make sure that the parcel was still there. The big parcel of strawberry-jam sandwiches, which he'd made the evening before.

His boots in his hand, Tommy tip-toed to the door where Norman was waiting, a rolled-up bundle in his arms.

"Ready?" Norman whispered, and Tommy nodded.

"Good lad," said Norman. "I've got candles and matches. And the table-cloths and blankets. I only hope this plan of yours works."

It was Tommy's plan which had finally made Norman change his mind and let Tommy come with them, providing Tommy stayed well out of the way if it came to a fight. Tommy had given his promise, because if things went the way he hoped, there wouldn't even *be* a fight.

Norman opened the door and they slipped out into the street. A dark figure moved towards them in the moonlight as they were fastening their boots.

"Albert?" whispered Norman. "Is that you?"

"Nah, it's Santa Claus," came the reply, and Tommy stifled a nervous giggle.

"Got the blankets, Norm?" the figure asked, coming closer.

"And the white tablecloths," replied Norman. "Me mam would have a fit if she knew I'd pinched her best linen. Did you bring the chalk?"

Albert pulled a handful of white lumps from his pocket. "Here it is," he said. "And I've told seven of the lads what we're up to. They'll be waiting at the gates when we come out."

"*If* we come out," said Norman, tucking his bundle more securely under his arm. "Right, then. Away we go."

Nobody was about, and they met no trouble as they made their way along the beach towards the caves. The sea gleamed silver in the moonlight, and Tommy wished they could just stand there and look at it for a while, instead of having to crawl into a horrible spooky tunnel with goodness-knows-what waiting at the other end.

"Getting cold feet?" asked Norman. Tommy gritted his teeth and took a deep breath, thinking of Gleam locked up in that dark cellar.

"Who me?" he squeaked. "Not likely!" He was first into the cave.

Norman lit a candle while Tommy and Albert rolled away the rock. Then, in the flickering light, they all stood and looked at the opening.

"*I'll* go first," said Norman, used to underground passages after working down the mine. Holding the candle in front, he crawled into the tunnel's dark mouth.

Tommy soon forgot to be scared when he found how easy it was. The smugglers had gone to a lot of trouble to smooth the rocky floor and walls, and

there was enough space for a man to
crawl along comfortably. The only
problem was the water, which dripped
from the roof and collected in puddles
on the floor.

After a few yards the tunnel began to
climb steeply upwards, and it was hard

to get a grip on the slippery rock. But by searching out cracks to get hold of, they managed to pull themselves slowly along.

Nobody spoke, and all they could hear was the drip of water and their own breathing. Then suddenly Tommy stopped, and listened hard.

"What was that?" he whispered, holding his breath. The noise came again, and this time there could be no mistake. It was the faint sound of horses whinnying not far ahead.

Tommy and the others scrambled

hastily on, and it wasn't long before they reached the tunnel's end. All three stared helplessly at one another for a moment, for in front of them was a blank wall of rock.

Norman held up the candle and examined the wall inch by inch.

"There must be a secret panel or something," he muttered. "Come on, you idle blighters. Help me look."

It was Tommy who found it. A tiny metal ring set into the wall near the floor.

"Look!" he said, his eyes round as ping-pong balls. "I bet that's it!"

Tommy grasped the ring and gave it a pull. Suddenly, with a slight rumble, a slab of rock slid neatly to one side. Crawling nervously through the opening, the lads found themselves in a cold, damp cellar.

To Tommy's joy, there were the ponies, huddled together in a corner in the dark. Startled at first by the light from the candle and the sudden appearance of three strange figures, they reared up and snorted in fright.

Norman stuck the candle into a crack in the wall. "Steady, now!" he said, patting the ponies' necks soothingly. "It's only us." And the ponies quickly calmed down and began to whinny with pleasure as they recognised their friends.

Tommy peered into the gloom, straining his eyes to see which of the ponies was Gleam. But Gleam found him first, and it was hard to tell who was the more delighted.

"Good lad, Gleam!" gulped Tommy, wiping his eyes on his sleeve, and turning his head away so the others wouldn't see. He fondled the pony's silky ears, and a great feeling of relief crept over him.

Looking for jam, Gleam began to nuzzle Tommy's pocket. But before Tommy could give him any, Norman had started up the wide stone steps to the cellar door.

"Come on," he said. "We've still got to get out of this place. And if Tommy's plan doesn't work, we're all done for."

He unrolled the bundle which he still had under his arm, and gave Tommy and Albert each an old grey army-blanket and a square white tablecloth.

Tommy had already cut a hole in the middle of each blanket so that it could be pulled over the head and worn like a long grey gown.

"I feel like a proper sissy," grumbled Albert, tying the gown round his skinny waist and draping the white cloth over his head. "I hope none of me mates see me like this."

Tommy, busy fixing his own costume, giggled so much that his tablecloth kept falling off.

"Never mind, Albert," he said. "You look great. Give us a bit of chalk."

Dressed in their dark grey gowns and white head-dresses, their faces and hands rubbed with chalk until they gleamed a ghostly white, the lads stood at the top of the cellar steps.

"Ready?" whispered Norman, and the other two nodded. "Right, now!" And all three began to sob and moan and wail in high-pitched voices.

It wasn't long before they heard the rattle of bolts being drawn back, and the cellar door was flung open.

"What the devil . . . ?" growled a rough voice, and Danny Bates stuck his head round the door.

Three robed and hooded figures

slowly glided past him, weeping and wailing and waving their hands.

Danny staggered back against the door. "*Aagh*, ghosts!" he howled. "It's them Three Sisters!"

The rest of the gang, rolled up in blankets and sleeping-bags on the floor of the great hall in front of a log fire,

leapt up and fell over themselves in confusion. Then they clung to one another and shrieked in fright as the firelight revealed three ghostly figures moving grimly towards them across the room.

"Help! I'm getting out of here!" roared one, grabbing his boots and making for the door, and it wasn't long before the others followed. Danny Bates himself led the way, his teeth chattering in terror and his face pale as a pancake in the darkness. The whole mob fled into the night, leaving the iron gates wide open.

"Them beggars won't come back in a hurry," murmured Norman. And Tommy and Albert grinned happily as they watched them go.

It was a gleeful procession that trotted back to the Banky Field a short

while later. It had taken no time at all
for the jubilant three to get out of their
costumes and bring the ponies up the
cellar steps and into the fresh air. The
other seven lads had kept their promise
and were waiting near the gates to ride
the ponies home.

They set off along the cliff-path in the
moonlight, Albert riding his favourite

black mare and Norman on his frisky grey.

In front of them all went Tommy, riding his beautiful Gleam, and leaning forward from time to time to put another strawberry-jam sandwich into the pony's mouth.

THE GHOST AT NO. 13
Gyles Brandreth

Hamlet Brown's sister, Susan, is just too perfect. Everything she does is praised and Hamlet is in despair – until a ghost comes to stay for a holiday and helps him to find an exciting idea for his school project!

RADIO DETECTIVE
John Escott

A piece of amazing deduction by the Roundbay Radio Detective when Donald, the radio's young presenter, solves a mystery but finds out more than anyone expects.

RAGDOLLY ANNA'S CIRCUS
Jean Kenward

Made only from a morsel of this and a tatter of that, Ragdolly Anna is a very special doll and the six stories in this book are all about her adventures.

SEE YOU AT THE MATCH
Margaret Joy

Six delightful stories about football. Whether spectator, player, winner or loser, these short, easy stories for young readers are a must for all football fans.

THREE LITTLE FUNNY ONES
Charlotte Hough

Oliver, Timmy and Tom are the funny ones, and they have some good adventures together, and some scary ones too. Like the time when the baby gets lost, or when the old cow thinks they are three mangold wurzels, or when they make a lion trap and catch a sausage dog.

THE HODGEHEG
Dick King-Smith

The story of Max, the hedgehog who becomes a hodgeheg, who becomes a hero. A delightfully original story from a master storyteller.

THE SCHOOL POOL GANG
Geraldine Kaye

Billy is the head of the Black Lane Gang, and he's always coming up with good ideas. So when money is needed for a new school pool, his first idea is to change the gang's name. His next idea leads to all sorts of unexpected and exciting happenings!